Lina the Shooting Star

Shooting Star

별 똥 별

리나

English-Korean compilation

서문

이 책은 지구로 떨어지며 기억을 잃은
별똥별 리나가 새로운 친구들을 만나고,
자신의 용기와 친구들의 도움으로
다시 자신의 별자리로 돌아가는 여정을 담고 있습니다.

별똥별 리나와 함께하는 이 여행은
어린이들에게 꿈과 희망을 선물하고,
어른들에게는 잃어버린 동심을 되찾아 줄 것입니다.

리나의 이야기를 떠올리며
별빛 가득한 밤하늘을 바라볼 때
여러분의 가슴 속에도 작은 별이
반짝이기를 바랍니다.

여러분의 꿈을 응원합니다.

별똥별 리나

작가 정영선

밤하늘이 반짝이던 어느 날
하늘에서 작은 별똥별이
지구로 떨어졌어요.

"소원을 빌면 이루어진대!"
마을의 아이들이 소리쳤죠.

"짹짹짹, 짹짹짹"
푹신한 풀밭에 누워 있던 리나는
새들의 지저귐에 눈을 떴어요.

눈앞에는 푸른 숲이 펼쳐져 있었지만
리나는 여기가 어디인지
자신이 누구인지 도통 기억나지 않았어요.

갑자기 빗방울이 떨어지기 시작했어요.
그때 귀여운 토끼가 나타나 말했어요.
"빨리 이리로 와! 내 굴로 피하면 돼!"

리나는 토끼를 따라 서둘러
토끼굴로 들어갔어요.
"비가 이렇게 갑자기 내리다니,
여긴 정말 신기한 곳이야."
리나는 중얼거렸어요.

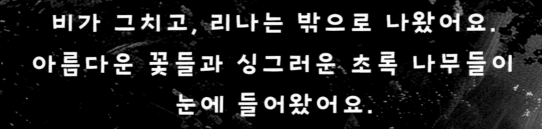

비가 그치고, 리나는 밖으로 나왔어요.
아름다운 꽃들과 싱그러운 초록 나무들이
눈에 들어왔어요.

"안녕? 여기가 어디야?
난 길을 잃었어."

토끼는 리나가 궁금해 하는 것들을
친절하게 알려주었어요.

리나는 동물 친구들도
많이 사귀었어요.

친구들 덕분에 외롭지 않고
안전하게 지낼 수 있었어요.
"이곳은 참 좋은 곳이야!"

리나는 아름다운 지구에서
친구들과 행복한 시간을 보냈어요

그러던 어느 날, 하늘이 어두워지는 것을 본 리나는
자신이 있어야 할 곳이 하늘임을 깨달았어요.

동물 친구들이 모여 리나를 둘러싸고
이야기를 나눴어요.
"하늘에서 떨어졌다고? 정말 신기해!"
리나는 동물 친구들에게
별나라 이야기를 들려주었어요.

"난 별나라로 돌아가고 싶어.
그런데 어떻게 해야 할까?"
친구들은 리나가 하늘로 돌아갈 수 있도록
도와주기로 했어요.
친구들의 격려로 리나는 용기를 얻었어요.

동물 친구들은 함께 고민하며 말했어요.
"우리, 여우에게 가보자.
여우는 똑똑하니까 답을 알지도 몰라."

친구들은 리나와 합께
여우를 찾아갔어요.

여우는 리나의 이야기를 듣고 말했어요.
"산 꼭대기에 오래된 천문대가 있어.
거기에서 답을 찾을 수 있을 거야."

"친구들아, 잘 있어! 고마워!"
리나는 친구들에게 작별 인사를 하고
산으로 향했어요.

강한 바람과 비를 만난 리나는 굳게 다짐했어요.
"난 할 수 있어. 포기하지 않을 거야!"

"이 강을 어떻게 건너지?"
리나는 큰 돌들을 발견하고 조심스레 강을 건넜어요.

"산 정상까지 가야 해. 그곳에 답이 있을 거야."
리나는 천천히 산을 오르기 시작했어요.

"어라, 길이 어디로 갔지?"
잠시 길을 잃은 리나는 주변을 둘러보며
길을 찾았어요.

밤이 되자 리나는 별들을
바라보며 속삭였어요.
"별들아, 제발 나를 집으로
돌아갈 수 있게 도와줘."

드디어 리나는 산꼭대기에 있는
천문대에 도착했어요.
"똑똑, 똑똑똑……"
리나는 천문대 문을 조심스럽게 두드렸어요.

문을 연 마법사는 미소를 지으며
리나를 맞이했어요.

"어서 오렴. 난 별에서 온 손님을 기다렸단다.
너의 용기와 친구들의 사랑이
네 꿈을 이룰 수 있게 도와줄 거란다."

마법사는 리나에게 별들의 비밀을
가르쳐 주었어요.

리나는 마법사와 함께 망원경으로
밤하늘을 관찰하며
자신의 별자리를 찾기 시작했어요.

"저기야! 저게 바로 내 별자리야!"
리나는 자신의 별자리를 발견하고 기뻐했어요.

마법사는 리나에게 마법의 망원경을 건네고
리나가 집으로 돌아갈 수 있게 준비했어요.

리나는 망원경을 들고 하늘로 통하는
길을 열었어요.
두근거리는 순간이었어요.

리나는 망원경을 통해 우주로 솟아올랐어요.
"마법사 할아버지, 안녕히 계세요.
또 놀러 올게요."

별들 사이로 날아가며
리나는 환호했어요.

자신의 별자리에 도착한 리나는
다시 빛나기 시작했어요.
"마침내, 집에 돌아왔어."

지구를 바라보며 리나는
친구들에게 감사를 전했어요.
"지구에서 배운 용기와 사랑 덕분에
난 더 밝게 빛날 수 있어."

리나는 별나라 친구들에게
자신의 모험 이야기를 들려주었어요.
"나는 지구에서 많은 걸 배웠어."

리나는 지구와 하늘에 꿈과 희망을 전했어요.
"내 꿈은 이루어졌어.
이제 나도 다른 이들의 소원을 들어줄 수 있어."

별똥별 리나가 기뻐하며 말했어요,
"모두들, 꿈을 잃지 마!"

Lina the Shooting Star

별똥별 리나

English-Korean compilation by Jeong young sun

Preface

This book tells the journey of a shooting star named Lina,
who loses her memory and falls to Earth.
Lina meets new friends and, with her courage
and the help of her friends,
finds her way back to the home.

Traveling with Lina will gift children dreams and hope,
and help adults rediscover their lost sense of wonder.

As you recall Lina's story and gaze at the star-filled night sky,
may a little star shine in your heart too.

I support your dreams.

Lina the Shooting Star
young-sun Jeong

One night when the sky was sparkling,
a small shooting star fell to Earth.

Make a wish, and it will come true!
shouted the children of the village.

"Chirp chirp, chirp chirp"
Lying on the soft grass,
Lina opened her eyes
to the sound of birds chirping.

In front of her was a vast green forest,
but Lina couldn't remember
where she was or who she was.

Suddenly, raindrops began to fall.
Just then, a cute rabbit appeared and said,
"Quickly, come here!
You can take shelter in my burrow!"

Lina hurriedly followed the rabbit into its burrow.
"It's amazing how the rain started so suddenly here."
Lina muttered.

After the rain stopped, Lina came out.
She was greeted by beautiful flowers
and fresh green trees.

"Hello? Where am I?
I'm lost."

The rabbit kindly explained everything
Lina was curious about.

Lina made many animal friends.
Thanks to them, she didn't feel lonely
and could stay safe.
"This place is wonderful!"

Lina spent happy times with her friends
on the beautiful Earth.

One day, seeing the sky darken,
Lina realized she belonged in the sky.

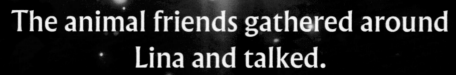

The animal friends gathered around
Lina and talked.
"You fell from the sky? How amazing!"
Lina told them stories about the star world.

"I want to return to the my home.
But how can I do it?"
Her friends decided to help
Lina get back to the sky.

Encouraged by her friends,
Lina gained courage.

The animal friends thought together and said,
"Let's go to the fox.
The fox is smart and might know the answer."

They all went to find the fox with Lina.

After hearing Lina's story, the fox said,
"There is an old observatory on the mountain peak.
You might find the answer there."

"Goodbye, my friends! Thank you!"
Lina said farewell and headed for the mountain.

Facing strong winds and rain, Lina resolved.
"I can do it. I won't give up!"

"How can I cross this river?"
Lina found some large stones
and carefully crossed the river.

"I have to get to the mountain top.
The answer must be there."
Lina began climbing the mountain slowly.

Oh no, where did the path go?
Momentarily lost, Lina looked around
and found the way.

At night, Lina gazed at the stars and whispered,
"Stars, please help me find my way home."

Finally, Lina arrived at the observatory
at the mountain peak.
"Knock, knock, knock...
" Lina gently knocked on the door.

The wizard opened the door
and welcomed Lina.

"Welcome, I have been waiting for a guest from the stars.
Your courage and the love of your friends will help you achieve your dream."

The wizard taught Lina the secrets of the stars.

Lina and the wizard began observing the night sky with the telescope, searching for her star.

"There it is! That's my star!"
Lina rejoiced upon finding her constellation.

The wizard handed Lina a magical telescope
and prepared her to return home.

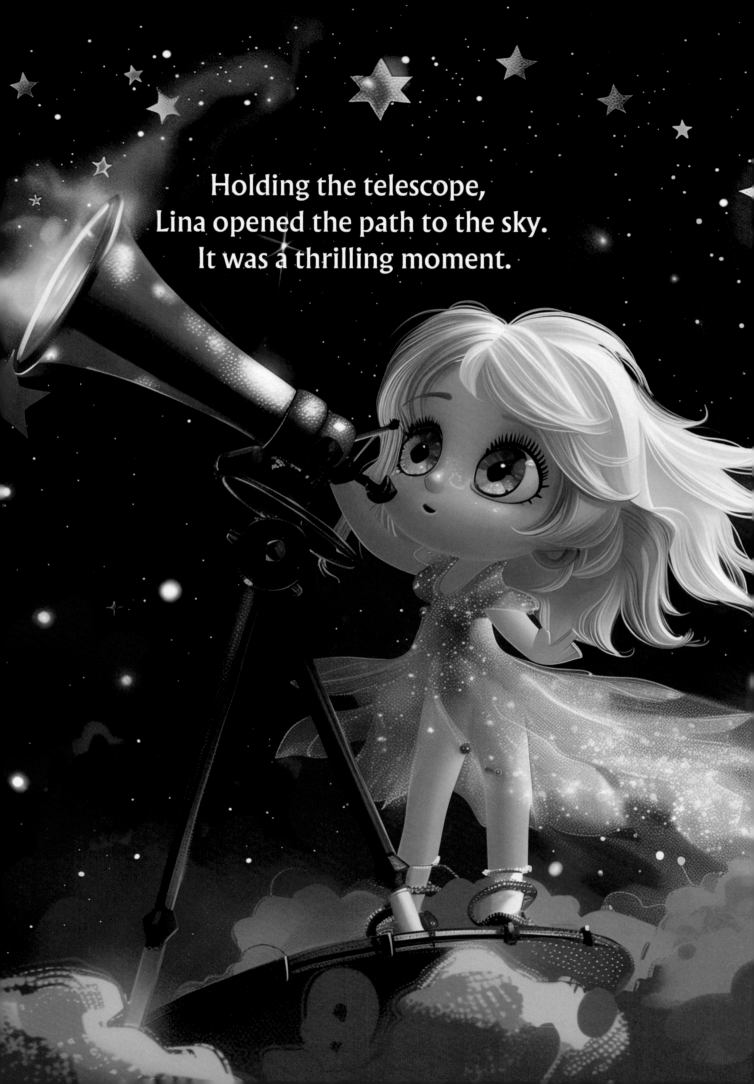

Holding the telescope,
Lina opened the path to the sky.
It was a thrilling moment.

Lina soared into space through the telescope.
"Goodbye, wizard. I'll come visit again."

Flying among the stars, Lina cheered.

Arriving at her constellation,
Lina began to shine again.
"Finally, I'm home."

Looking at Earth, Lina thanked her friends.
"Thanks to the courage and love I learned on Earth,
I can shine brighter."

Lina shared her adventure stories
with her star friends.
"I learned so much on Earth."

Lina spread dreams and hope
to both Earth and the sky.
"My dream came true.
Now I can grant others' wishes too."

Lina the shooting star said joyfully,
"Everyone, never lose your dreams!"

I support your dreams.

Lina the Shooting Star
young-sun Jeong

별똥별 리나 (한영 합본)
Lina the Shooting Star (Korean-English compilation)

발 행 | 2024년 8월 2일

저 자 | 정영선

펴낸이 | 한건희

펴낸곳 | 주식회사 부크크

출판사등록 | 2014.07.15.(제2014-16호)

주 소 | 서울특별시 금천구 가산디지털1로 119

SK트윈타워 A동 305호

전 화 | 1670-8316

이메일 | INFO@BOOKK.CO.KR

ISBN | 979-11-410-9930-5

WWW.BOOKK.CO.KR